PLEASE DON'T SING!

A story about the power of the human spirit

by

Meritta S. White

Illustrated by Omot Akway

Dedicated

to

Alton and Corean White

A true measure of a father and mother's devotion and sacrifice is a grateful daughter.

Thank you!

AND

To the lost loved ones and survivors of the world's natural disasters.

Songbirds love to sing.

So does P'ngh (pronounced "Ping").

This is P'ngh. P'ngh loves to sing.

But NOBODY likes to hear P'ngh sing.

No one in the stores

or behind closed doors—

NOBODY likes to hear P'ngh sing. Because...

P'ngh sings loudly,

off-key,

and sometimes

inappropriately.

Whenever P'ngh sings, people SAY:

"P'ngh, please don't sing!"

No one in the mountains,

in the valley,

in the hillsides, or

in the alley—

NOBODY likes to hear P'ngh sing.

But P'ngh is happy—

So P'ngh sings in the rain,

in the snow,

in the sunshine,

EVEN THOUGH—

People SHOUT:

don't sing!!"

But NOBODY knows...

P'ngh cannot hear a thing and
does not quite know how to sing.
P'ngh has never heard a song to sing.

But P'ngh is happy—

So each day P'ngh sings

loudly,

off-key,

and sometimes

inappropriately.

And everyday people SCREAM:

DON'T SING!!!"

One day the earth shook.
Buildings swayed and fell.
Everywhere was quiet.

Then a voice was heard.
It was loud, off-key and UNWAVERING.

"Could that be P'ngh?"
"Would P'ngh dare to sing...NOW?"

Everybody listened.
NOBODY said, "P'ngh, please don't sing!"
Everybody grew calm.

Soon the searchers came and rescued everybody.

But then...

Someone noticed that P'ngh no longer had a song to sing.

"P'ngh, please sing," everyone pleaded.

But P'ngh **WOULD NOT** sing.

P'ngh **COULD NOT** sing.

Songbirds sing more frequently in the spring.

And each spring **EVERYBODY** remembers P'ngh and sings...

loudly,

off-key,

and **EVEN** inappropriately!

Songbirds love to sing.

So did P'ngh!

The End